My dear Rose,

After leaving the planet of the Tortoise Driver, I treasure our correspondence even more, not just so I can tell you my adventures, but so I can find out how you're doing.

The Snake tried once again to keep people from communicating, and Fox and I were hard-pressed to stop him!

Our journey leads us to all sorts of planets, and whatever their differences may be, we have found that almost all their problems are due to a lack of communication, whether because of hostility or fear! And when people stop communicating, it's not just individual relationships that suffer, but the whole society starts to collapse.

The Little Prince

First American edition published in 2013 by Graphic Universe™.

Le Petit Prince ™

based on the masterpiece by Antoine de Saint-Exupéry

© 2013 LPPM
An animated series based on the novel *Le Petit Prince* by Antoine de Saint-Exupéry
Developed for television by Matthieu Delaporte, Alexandre de la Patellière, and Bertrand Gatignol
Directed by Pierre-Alain Chartier

© 2013 ÉDITIONS GLÉNAT
Copyright © 2013 by Lerner Publishing Group, Inc., for the current edition

Graphic Universe™
A division of Lerner Publishing Group, Inc.
241 First Avenue North
Minneapolis, MN 55401 U.S.A.

Website address : www.lernerbooks.com

Library of Congress Cataloging-in-Publication Data

Bruneau, Clotilde.
   [Planète du Géant. English]
   The planet of the Giant / story by Gilles Adrien and Alain Broders ; design and illustrations by Élyum Studio ; adapted by Clotilde Bruneau ; translation, Anne Collins Smith and Owen Smith. — 1st American ed.
      p.   cm. — (The little prince ; #09)
   ISBN 978—0—7613—8759—6 (lib. bdg. : alk. paper)
   ISBN 978—1—4677—1652—9 (eBook)
   1. Graphic novels. I. Smith, Anne Collins, translator. II. Smith, Owen (Owen M.), translator. III. Adrien, Gilles. IV. Broders, Alain. V. Saint-Exupéry, Antoine de, 1900—1944. Petit Prince. VI. Élyum Studio. VII. Petit Prince (Television program) VIII. Title.
PZ7.7.B8Pl 2013
741.5'944—dc23   2013000319

Manufactured in the United States of America
1 — DP — 7/15/13

THE NEW ADVENTURES
BASED ON THE MASTERPIECE BY ANTOINE DE SAINT-EXUPÉRY

The Little Prince

THE PLANET OF THE GIANT

Based on the animated series and an original story by Gilles Adrien & Alain Broders

Design: Elyum Studio
Story: Clotilde Bruneau
Artistic Direction: Didier Poli
Art: Audrey Bussi
Backgrounds: Isa Python
Coloring: Karine Lambin
Editing: Didier Poli
Editorial Consultant: Didier Convard

Translation: Anne and Owen Smith

Graphic Universe™ • Minneapolis

THE LITTLE PRINCE

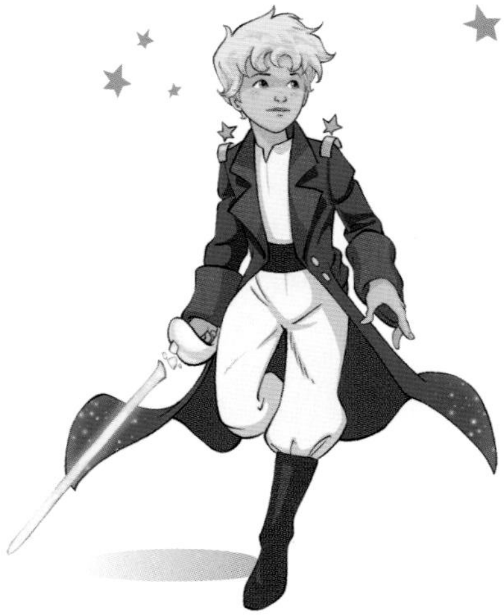

The Little Prince has extraordinary gifts. His sense of wonder allows him to discover what no one else can see. The Little Prince can communicate with all the beings in the universe, even the animals and plants. His powers grow over the course of his adventures.

The Prince's uniform:
When he transforms into the uniform of a prince, he is more agile and quick. When faced with difficult situations, the Little Prince also uses a sword that lets him sketch and bring to life anything from his imagination.

His sketchbook:
When he is not in his Prince's clothing, the Little Prince carries a sketchbook. When he blows on the pages, they take wing and form objects that he'll find very useful. Like his sword, it's powered by stardust collected on his travels.

FOX

A grouch, a trickster, and, so he says, interested only in his next meal, Fox is in reality the Little Prince's best friend. As such, he is always there to give him help but also just as much to help him to grow and to learn about the world.

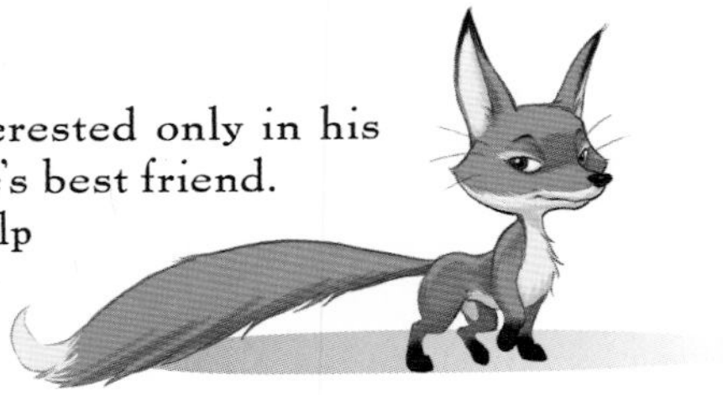

THE SNAKE

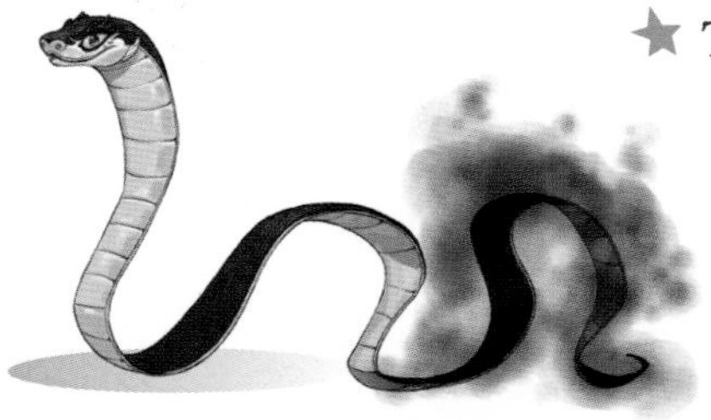

Even though the Little Prince still does not know exactly why, there can be no doubt that the Snake has set his mind to plunging the entire universe into darkness! And to accomplish his goal, this malicious being is ready to use any form of deception. However, the Snake never takes action himself. He prefers to bring out the wickedness in those beings he has chosen to bite, tempting them to put their own worlds in danger.

THE GLOOMIES

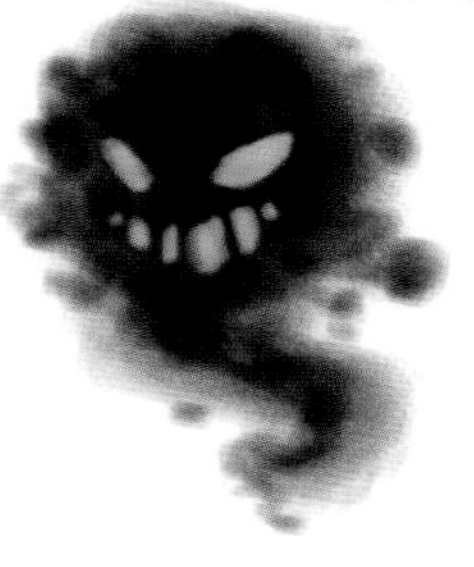

When people who have been "bitten" by the Snake have completely destroyed their own planets, they become Gloomies, slaves to their Snake master. The Gloomies act as a group and carry out the Snake's most vile orders so he can get the better of the Little Prince!

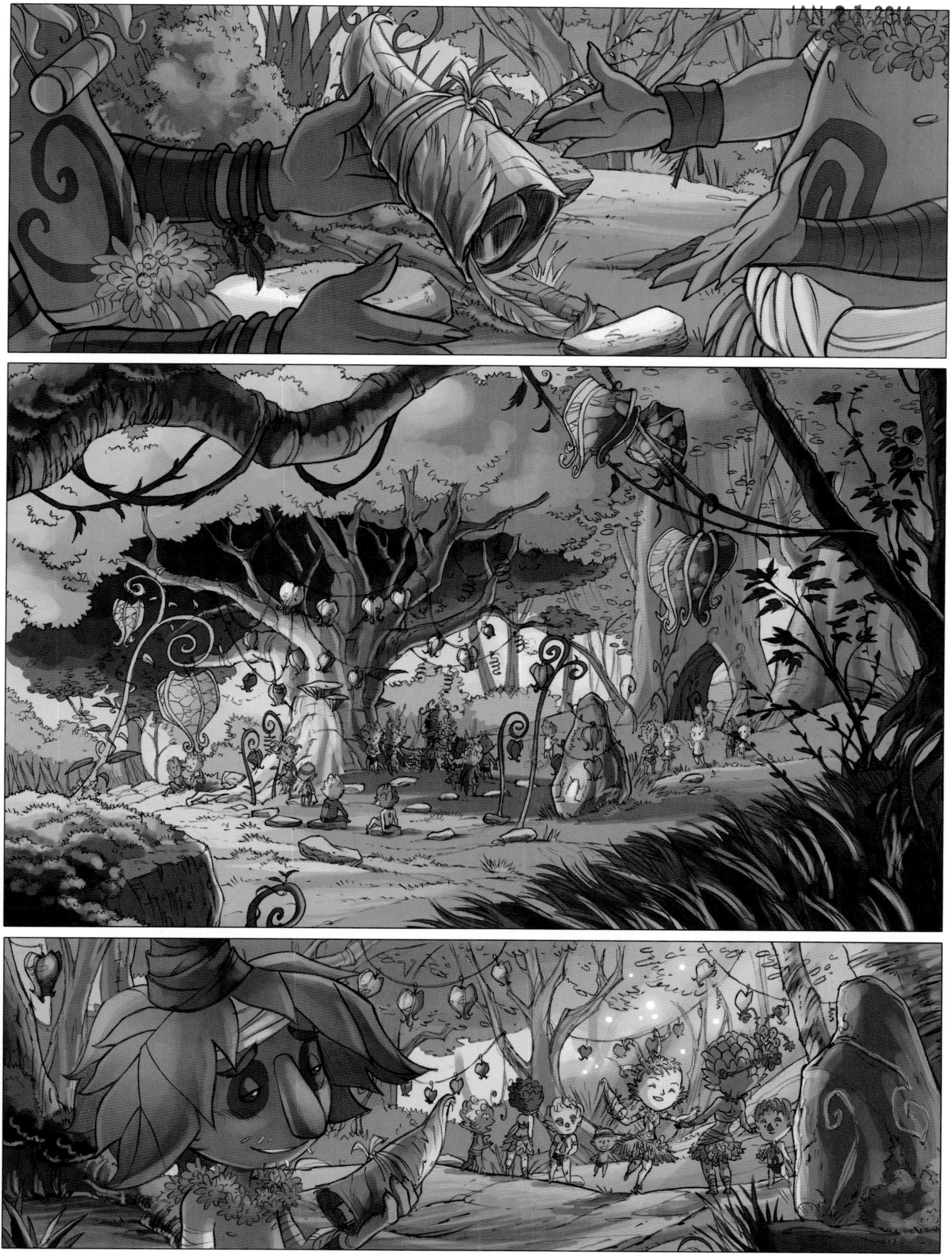

SO, TALAMUS, YOU PLACED FIRST IN EVERY SUBJECT AT SCHOOL! YOU'RE GOING TO MAKE A GREAT MASTERMIND! WHEN DOES YOUR APPRENTICESHIP BEGIN?

I START NEXT WEEK! I MUST ADMIT I'M A BIT SCARED OF WORKING ALL BY MYSELF.

TRY NOT TO WORRY. BESIDES, YOU KNOW THE RULE: THE TOP STUDENT ALWAYS WORKS WITH THE BRAIN!

BACK TO MY ROUNDS. KEEP UP THE GOOD WORK!

WAIT!

UM... NATURA... SHE GOT GOOD GRADES, DIDN'T SHE? WILL SHE BE THE SUPERVISOR?

I'M SURE YOU'LL FIND A WAY TO STAY IN TOUCH!

CLICK DID JUST A LITTLE BETTER, SO HE'LL BE THE SUPERVISOR! NATURA IS GOING TO BE IN CHARGE OF THE SCHOOL!

WOW, THAT'S AN AWESOME SONG! YOU'RE REALLY TALENTED!

OH, NATURA, BEAUTY OF MY HEART...

COUGH COUGH... ANOTHER FINE LANDFALL.

NYAHHH!

THANK YOU, FOX. I COULDN'T USE MY POWERS UNDER THE SAND...COUGH COUGH... IT LOOKS LIKE WE LANDED ON A DESERT PLANET!

ARE YOU SURE?

WOW!

HM...
THIS PLANET'S
PROBLEM IS
OBVIOUS.
SOMETHING'S
WRONG WITH THE
CLIMATE.

DO YOU
HEAR THAT NOISE?
IT SOUNDS LIKE
PEOPLE ARE
HOLDING A PARTY
UNDERGROUND!

THERE
MUST BE A
SUBTERRANEAN
CITY...WE MUST
FIND A WAY
TO GET DOWN
THERE!

BOOM
BOOM
BOOM
BOOM
BOOM
BOOM

PFFT! THE
KITCHENS WOULD
HAVE TO BE
UNDERGROUND...
DINNER'S
NOWHERE IN
SIGHT.

MAYBE IT
IS! FOR ONCE,
FOX, YOU SEEM
TO BE IN
LUCK!

A WOOD-
CLUCKER! THIS
PLANET IS FULL
OF SURPRISES!

HAVE YOU
FIGURED OUT
HOW TO CATCH
HER?

CLUCK-CLUCK?

JUST YOU WAIT UNTIL MY FAMOUS HUNTING INSTINCTS KICK IN!

HA HA! I BELIEVE YOU.

CLUCK! CLUCKCLUCKCLUCK CLUCK!

BUT...WHAT'S SHE DOING! I'M THE ONE WHO SHOULD BE CHASING *HER!*

CLUCK... CLUCKCLUCK CLUCK!

THAT BIRD'S GONE CUCKOO!

SHE'S AS MAD AS A... WET HEN! HA HA HA!!!

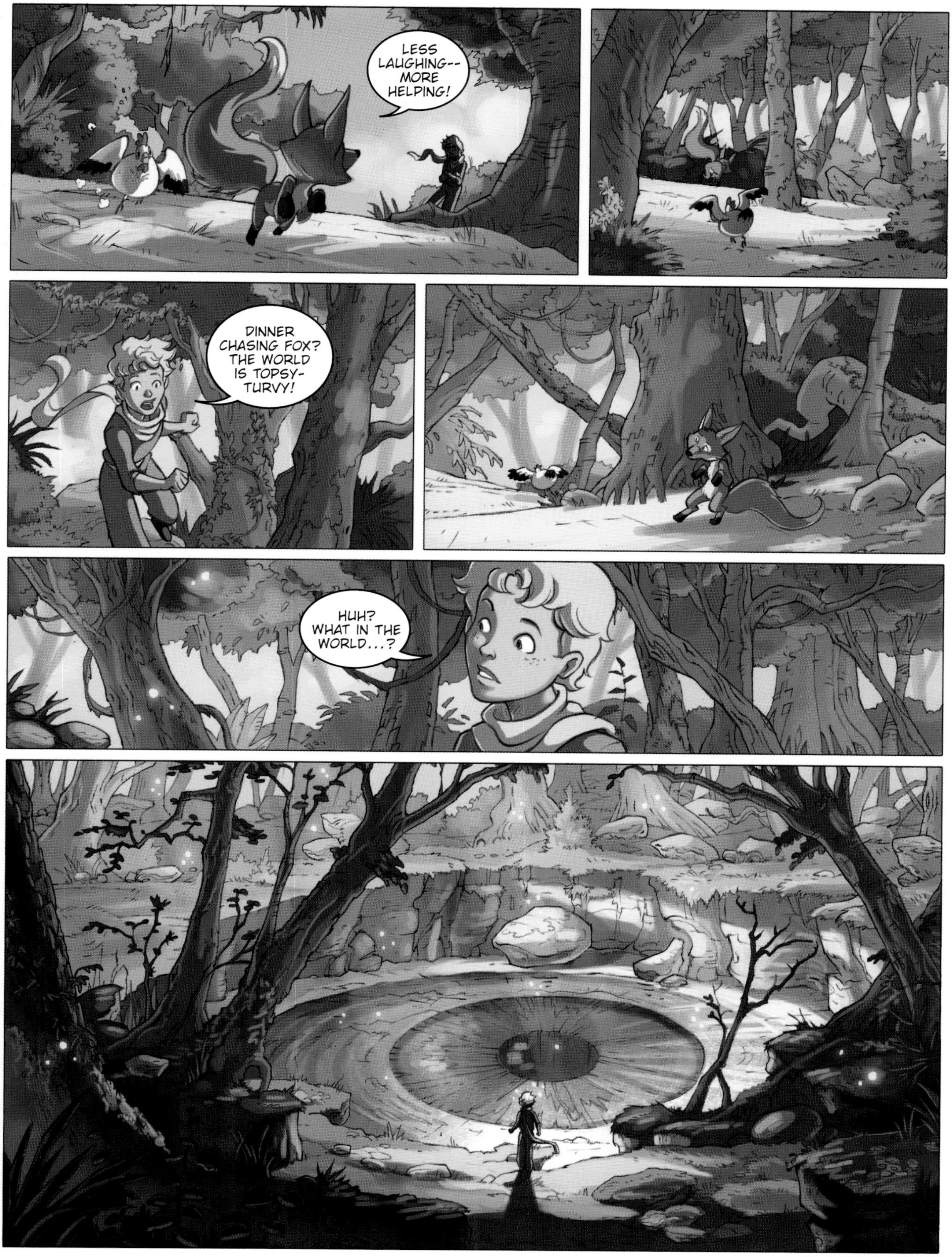
LESS LAUGHING-- MORE HELPING!
DINNER CHASING FOX? THE WORLD IS TOPSY-TURVY!
HUH? WHAT IN THE WORLD...?

YOU WEREN'T MUCH HELP! HAPPILY, MY CRAFTINESS KNOWS NO BOUNDS.

COME ON, FOX, I KNEW YOU HAD THE PLUCK TO ESCAPE!

WELL, THIS TURN OF EVENTS HAS GIVEN ME QUITE A THIRST!

AT LEAST DOWN HERE, I WON'T MEET ANY LOONEY BIRDS!

BLEAH! IT'S TOO SALTY! SOMETHING'S DEFINITELY NOT RIGHT HERE!

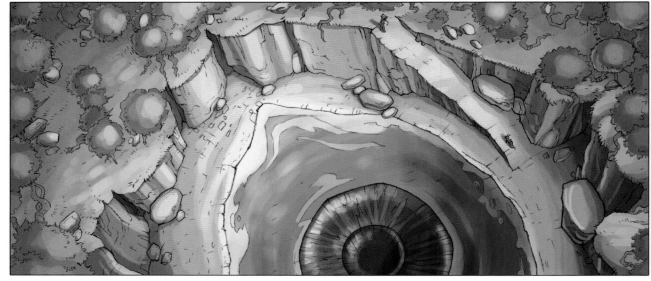

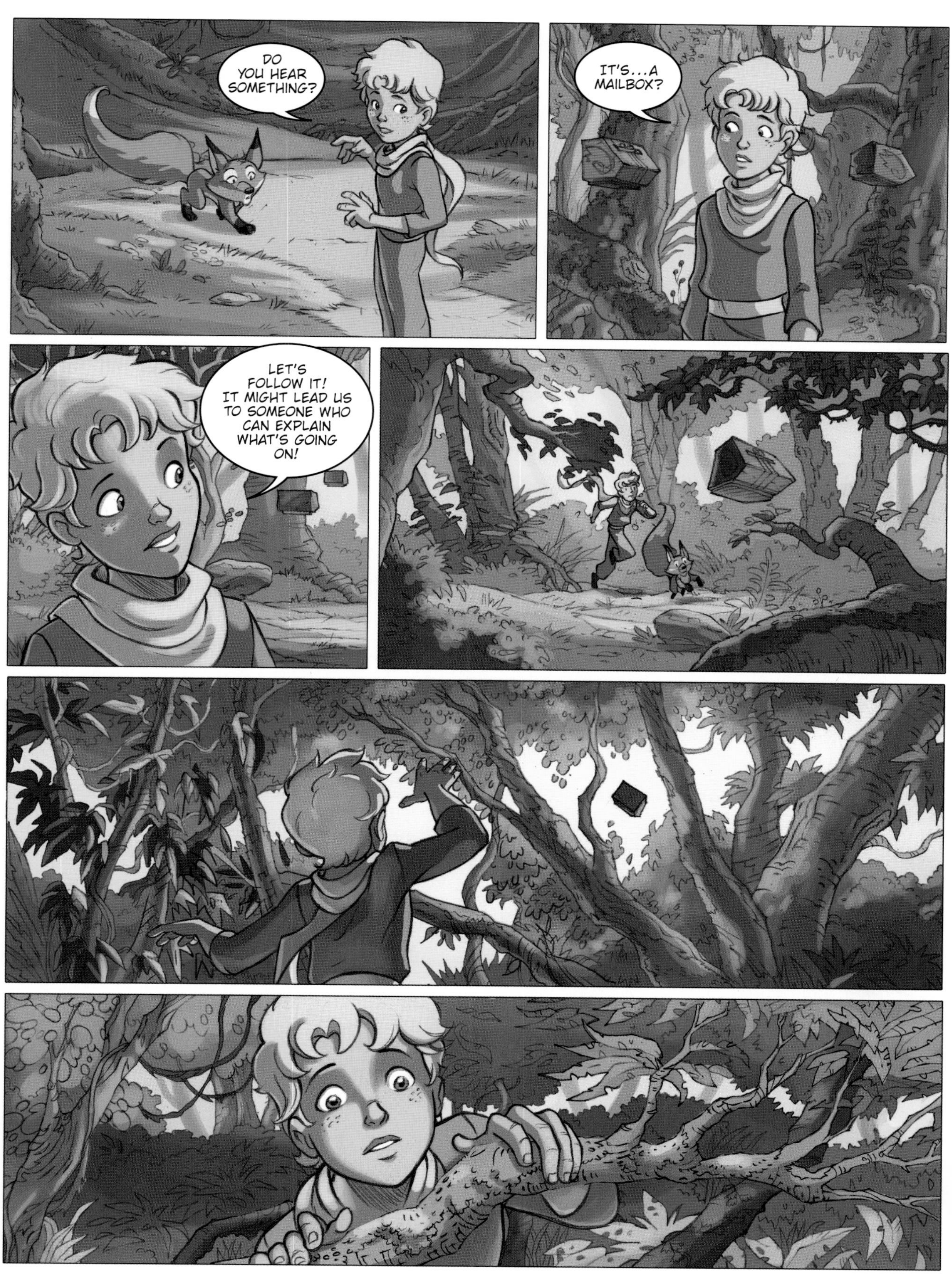
DO YOU HEAR SOMETHING?
IT'S...A MAILBOX?
LET'S FOLLOW IT! IT MIGHT LEAD US TO SOMEONE WHO CAN EXPLAIN WHAT'S GOING ON!

AND THAT'S WHY OUR GIANT...?

OOPS...

OOH, A FOX! IT'S SO CUTE!

CAN I HAVE A HUG?

WHY DOES EVERYONE HERE FIND ME SO ATTRACTIVE?

DON'T SCARE THE FOX, CHILDREN! CLASS DISMISSED! ...HELLO, I'M NATURA. CAN I HELP YOU?

UM...COULD YOU TELL HIM TO LET ME GO?

HELLO, I AM THE LITTLE PRINCE, AND THIS IS MY FRIEND FOX. WE JUST ARRIVED ON YOUR WORLD. WHAT A BEAUTIFUL PLACE!

NOT REALLY... WE TRAVEL FROM PLANET TO PLANET, TRYING TO HELP PEOPLE!

I WISH WE *WERE* ON VACATION!

YES, OUR ECOSYSTEM OPERATES UNDER VERY STRICT RULES. STILL, WE'VE BECOME VERY CONCERNED RECENTLY ABOUT ITS FRAGILE BALANCE. ARE YOU HERE ON VACATION?

SO...YOU'RE HERE TO HELP THE GIANT?

WELL, WE'RE A BIT CONCERNED ABOUT SOME THINGS ON YOUR PLANET, BUT WE DON'T KNOW ANYTHING ABOUT A GIANT...

WITH MY LUCK, HE'S GOING TO WANT TO HUG ME TOO!

LET ME EXPLAIN... OUR PLANET IS A GIANT LIVING BEING. EVERYONE HERE PLAYS A ROLE IN HELPING IT FUNCTION PROPERLY.

WELL, WE'VE BEEN WORRIED ABOUT TALAMUS FOR A WHILE. HE'S OUR MASTERMIND, THE ONE IN CHARGE OF THE PLANET'S BRAIN, AND HE HASN'T BEEN ANSWERING OUR MESSAGES.

SO, THIS GIANT IS NOT FEELING WELL?

WITHOUT ORDERS FROM THE PLANET'S BRAIN, THE ORGANS DO WHATEVER THEY PLEASE! WE'VE EVEN HAD EARTHQUAKES...

NATURA, I THINK I KNOW WHO IS BEHIND ALL THESE PROBLEMS...WE MUST CONTACT TALAMUS IMMEDIATELY TO NURSE THE GIANT BACK TO HEALTH! SINCE HE WON'T ANSWER YOUR CALLS, WE MUST VISIT HIM IN PERSON!

I THOUGHT OF THAT, BUT IT'S FORBIDDEN! BESIDES, IT WOULD TAKE US DAYS TO WALK THERE.

IT'S TIME TO BREAK THE RULES, NATURA! I CAN GET US THERE MUCH FASTER.

LOOK...

IT'S THE MAILBOX WE SAW EARLIER...THE GLOOMIES ARE ATTACKING IT!

WE'RE ALMOST THERE!

AAAAH!

WHAT'S HAPPPPENING??!

HUH?

IS EVERYONE OKAY?

IT'S YOU, NATURA! WHO AUTHORIZED AN EMERGENCY LANDING IN THE LUNGS? NO ONE SAID ANYTHING TO ME...

I'M SORRY, CLICK! THE GIANT INHALED US...WE WERE ON OUR WAY TO THE BRAIN. I HAD FORGOTTEN HOW DANGEROUS THE JOURNEY IS!

HEY--I HAVE AN IDEA! AS THE SUPERVISOR, YOU SHOULD KNOW A SAFE ROUTE TO THE BRAIN. TAKE US TO TALAMUS!

HOW CAN YOU SUGGEST SUCH A THING, NATURA? NO ONE CAN GO TO THE BRAIN WITHOUT AUTHORIZATION!

BUT TALAMUS HASN'T ANSWERED ANY MESSAGES SINCE--

HE ANSWERS *ME!* STILL, I MUST ADMIT HIS ANSWERS MAKE NO SENSE.

THE GIANT IS GOING FROM BAD TO WORSE. IF WE DON'T DO SOMETHING, THE PLANET WILL DIE... SINCE THE RULES ARE SO IMPORTANT TO YOU, SEND AN OFFICIAL REQUEST TO TALAMUS!

HM, I SUPPOSE I COULD DO THAT...

BRING ME A MAILBOX!

YOU'RE MAKING THE RIGHT DECISION, CLICK.

HERE'S THE MAILBOX, BOSS!

THERE'S NOTHING TO DO NOW BUT WAIT!

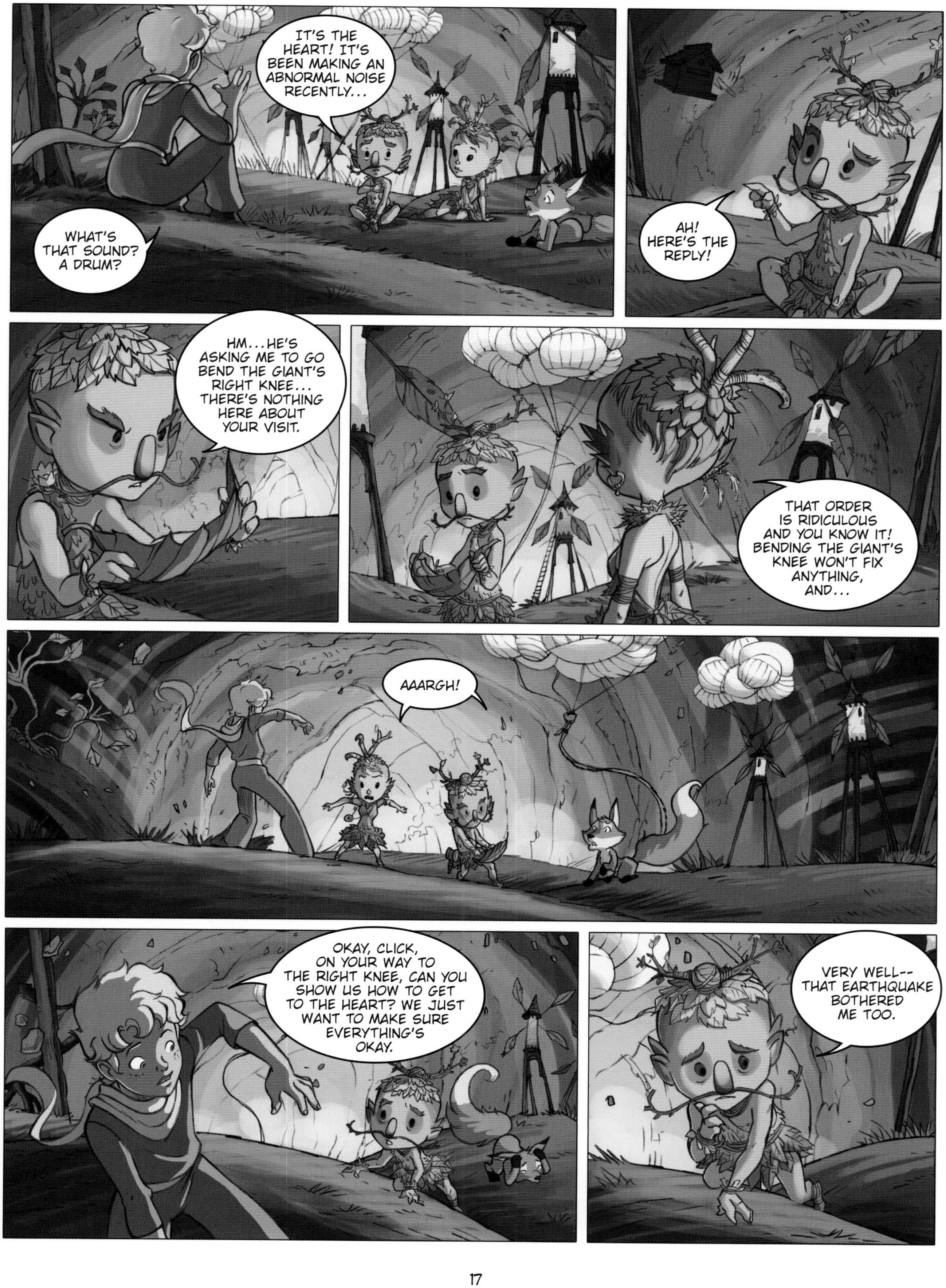
IT'S THE HEART! IT'S BEEN MAKING AN ABNORMAL NOISE RECENTLY...
WHAT'S THAT SOUND? A DRUM?
AH! HERE'S THE REPLY!
HM...HE'S ASKING ME TO GO BEND THE GIANT'S RIGHT KNEE... THERE'S NOTHING HERE ABOUT YOUR VISIT.
THAT ORDER IS RIDICULOUS AND YOU KNOW IT! BENDING THE GIANT'S KNEE WON'T FIX ANYTHING, AND...
AAARGH!
OKAY, CLICK, ON YOUR WAY TO THE RIGHT KNEE, CAN YOU SHOW US HOW TO GET TO THE HEART? WE JUST WANT TO MAKE SURE EVERYTHING'S OKAY.
VERY WELL-- THAT EARTHQUAKE BOTHERED ME TOO.

LUMINOUS...
NATURA...

ANOTHER INCOMING MESSAGE? MAYBE SOMETHING'S WRONG. I SHOULD GO--

NONSSSENSE, TALAMUSSSS... YOU HAVE BETTER THINGS TO DO! YOU MUST WRITE YOUR POEMS... HSS...

HSS...A GREAT POET LIKE YOU MUST CONSSSENTRATE ON HIS CREATIONSSSS. DO NOT ALLOW TRIVIAL MESSSSAGES TO DISTURB YOU!

I KNOW I NEED TO WRITE... BUT WHAT IF THERE'S A PROBLEM?

CALM YOURSELF, TALAMUSSS. IF ANYTHING WAS SSSERIOUSLY WRONG, YOU'D BE GETTING MESSAGES FROM THE WHOLE PLANET, NOT JUST CLICK! FOCUSSS ON YOUR TRUE CALLING...POETRY!

DON'T FORGET, COMPOSING THE PERFECT POEM IS THE ONLY WAY TO WIN NATURA'S HEART!

AAAH, NATURA...

YESSSS... WITH *YOUR* TALENT, YOU CAN DO EVEN BETTER!

LET'S GO, LITTLE PRINCE. WE CAN TAKE MY VELOCIPEDE!

UH, CLICK, I DON'T KNOW THESE ROUTES AS WELL AS YOU DO, BUT ARE YOU SURE WE'RE GOING THE RIGHT WAY? THE AIR DOESN'T SMELL RIGHT...

NONSENSE, NATURA! AFTER ALL, WE FOLLOWED THE SIGNS!

AND WE HAVE TO TRUST THEM. WITHOUT THE SIGNS, WE'D BE COMPLETELY LOST!

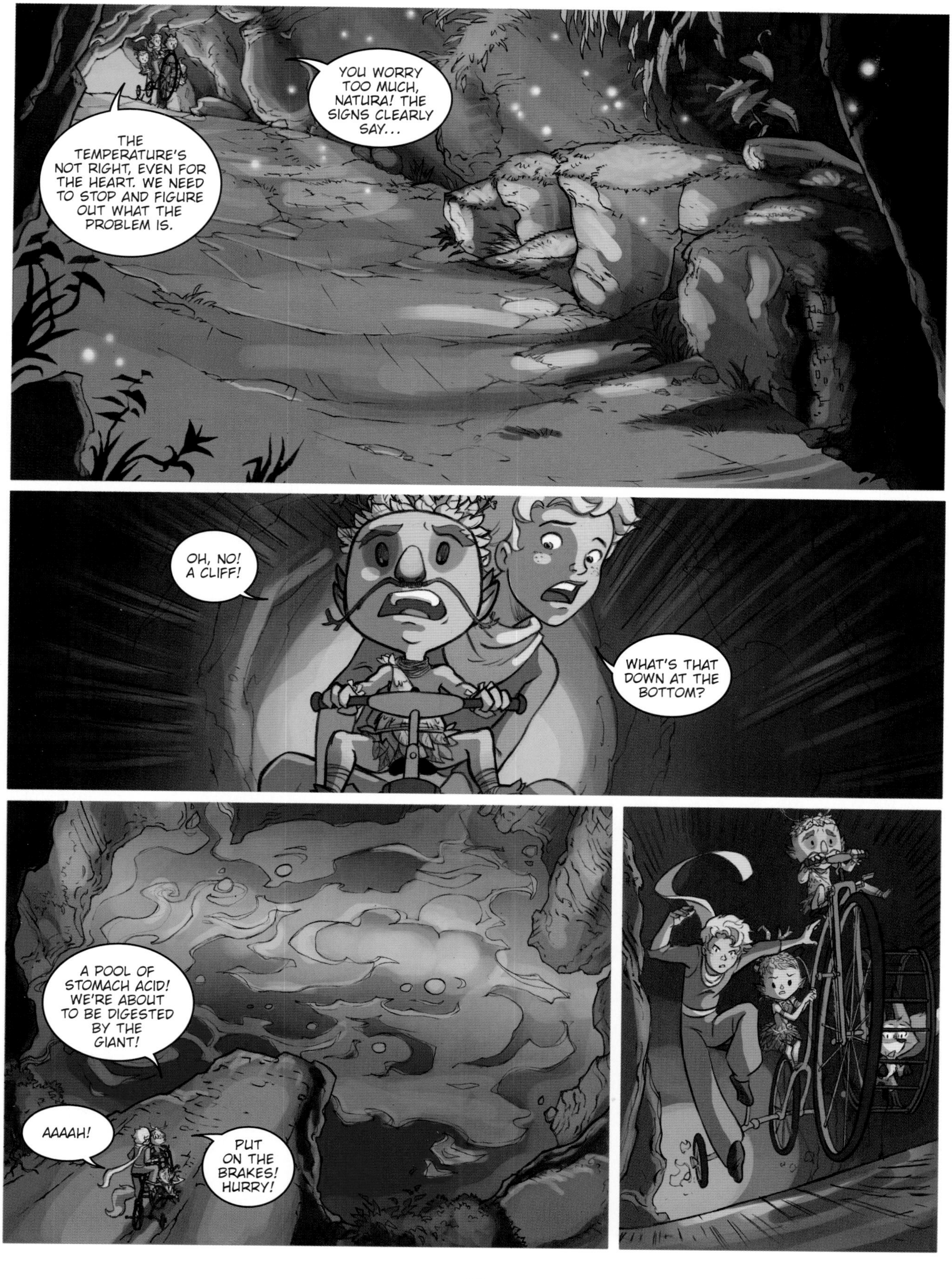
THE TEMPERATURE'S NOT RIGHT, EVEN FOR THE HEART. WE NEED TO STOP AND FIGURE OUT WHAT THE PROBLEM IS.
YOU WORRY TOO MUCH, NATURA! THE SIGNS CLEARLY SAY...
OH, NO! A CLIFF!
WHAT'S THAT DOWN AT THE BOTTOM?
A POOL OF STOMACH ACID! WE'RE ABOUT TO BE DIGESTED BY THE GIANT!
AAAAH!
PUT ON THE BRAKES! HURRY!

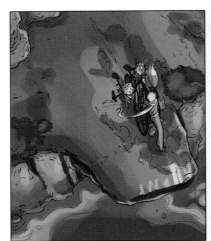

THAT WAS CLOSE! JUST THINK--I WOULDN'T HAVE *HAD* DINNER-- I WOULD HAVE *BEEN* DINNER!

WE'RE STILL IN DANGER! THE AIR IS TOO ACIDIC. WE CAN'T HOLD OUT FOR LONG!

I KNOW HOW WE CAN GET OUT OF HERE.

THAT'S THE LAST THING WE NEED!

WE HAVE TO JUMP INTO THESE BEADS OF SWEAT!

CLICK! YOU ALMOST GOT US KILLED BY BEING MR. "I HAVE TO FOLLOW THE RULES"!

HOW COULD I HAVE KNOWN THAT THE SIGNS WERE WRONG? I'VE NEVER HEARD OF SUCH A THING...

WHAT'S HAPPPPENING NOW?

LOOK AROUND YOU! DESERT EVERYWHERE, MORE AND MORE VIOLENT EARTHQUAKES...YOU MUST LEAD US TO THE BRAIN!

YES, BUT...

IF SOMETHING HAS HAPPENED TO TALAMUS, YOUR PLANET IS IN GRAVE DANGER. WE HAVE TO ACT NOW!

FOR ORDERS TO BE VALID, THEY MUST COME FROM TALAMUS, RIGHT?

SO AN OBEDIENT SUBORDINATE WOULD ACTUALLY DOUBLE-CHECK HIS ORDERS AND--

CLUCK CLUCK!

HELP!

OH NO!

CLUCK? CLUCK!

WHAT...?

OH, NO! LOOK--THE MAILBOXES!

THIS IS THE WORK OF THE GLOOMIES... THINGS ARE WORSE THAN I THOUGHT!

THIS IS A CATASTROPHE! NONE OF OUR MESSAGES HAVE GOTTEN THROUGH TO TALAMUS...UNLESS WE DO SOMETHING, IN A FEW HOURS THE GIANT WILL BECOME ONE HUGE DESERT!

DON'T GIVE UP HOPE, NATURA. THERE MUST BE A SOLUTION!

CLICK, IF TALAMUS ISN'T GETTING ANY MESSAGES, THE CHAIN OF COMMAND IS BROKEN, RIGHT?

LET ME THINK... IF WE LINK THE CURRENT DYSFUNCTIONALITY WITH EMERGENCY PROTOCOLS, WE HAVE AUTHORIZATION TO GO SEE TALAMUS IN PERSON.

OF COURSE! THERE MUST BE EMERGENCY PROCEDURES IN CASE OF A BREAKDOWN IN THE CHAIN OF COMMAND!

BEFORE WE LEAVE, HOWEVER, I AM REQUIRED TO SEND A MESSAGE INFORMING TALAMUS THAT MESSAGES ARE NO LONGER GETTING THROUGH!

SOOOO. TO TALAMUS FROM CLICK...

WAIT--I FEEL INSPIRATION IS ABOUT TO STRIKE!

IT'S JUST ANOTHER MESSSAGE FROM CLICK. HE DOESN'T SEEM TO BE VERY GOOD AT HIS JOB, DOES HE?

NO! HE JUST WANTS TO DISTRACT YOU. YOU CAN'T LET HIM COME HERE. HE'LL KEEP YOU FROM FINISHING YOUR POEM...YOU'RE ALMOSSST DONE!

HE SEEMS WORRIED. HE WANTS TO MEET WITH ME IN PERSON!

WITH A TALENT LIKE YOURS, ANY INTERRUPTION WOULD BE A CRIME AGAINST THE ART OF POETRY.

ALL I WANT TO DO IS TO WRITE POETRY...BUT HOW CAN I GET RID OF CLICK WITHOUT BEING RUDE?

GIVE HIM ANOTHER ASSIGNMENT ON THE OTHER SIDE OF THE GIANT'S BODY! THAT WILL KEEP HIM BUSY FOR A FEW HOURS-- LONG ENOUGH FOR YOU TO FINISH YOUR POEM!

YOU'RE RIGHT! THERE'S NOTHING SERIOUSLY WRONG WITH THE GIANT.

IT'S ONLY FOR A FEW HOURS...I'M NOT REALLY NEGLECTING MY DUTY.

I WONDER, THOUGH, WHY I HAVEN'T GOTTEN ANY MESSAGES FROM THE GIANT'S FEET FOR SEVERAL DAYS.

HSSS...PERHAPS YOU'LL BE INSPIRED TO WRITE A FEW MORE LINES BY TELLING ME AGAIN ABOUT YOUR POETIC MUSE...

AHHH, NATURA!

IT WAS THE SPRING BALL, AND I HAD BEEN IN LOVE WITH NATURA FOR A LONG TIME...

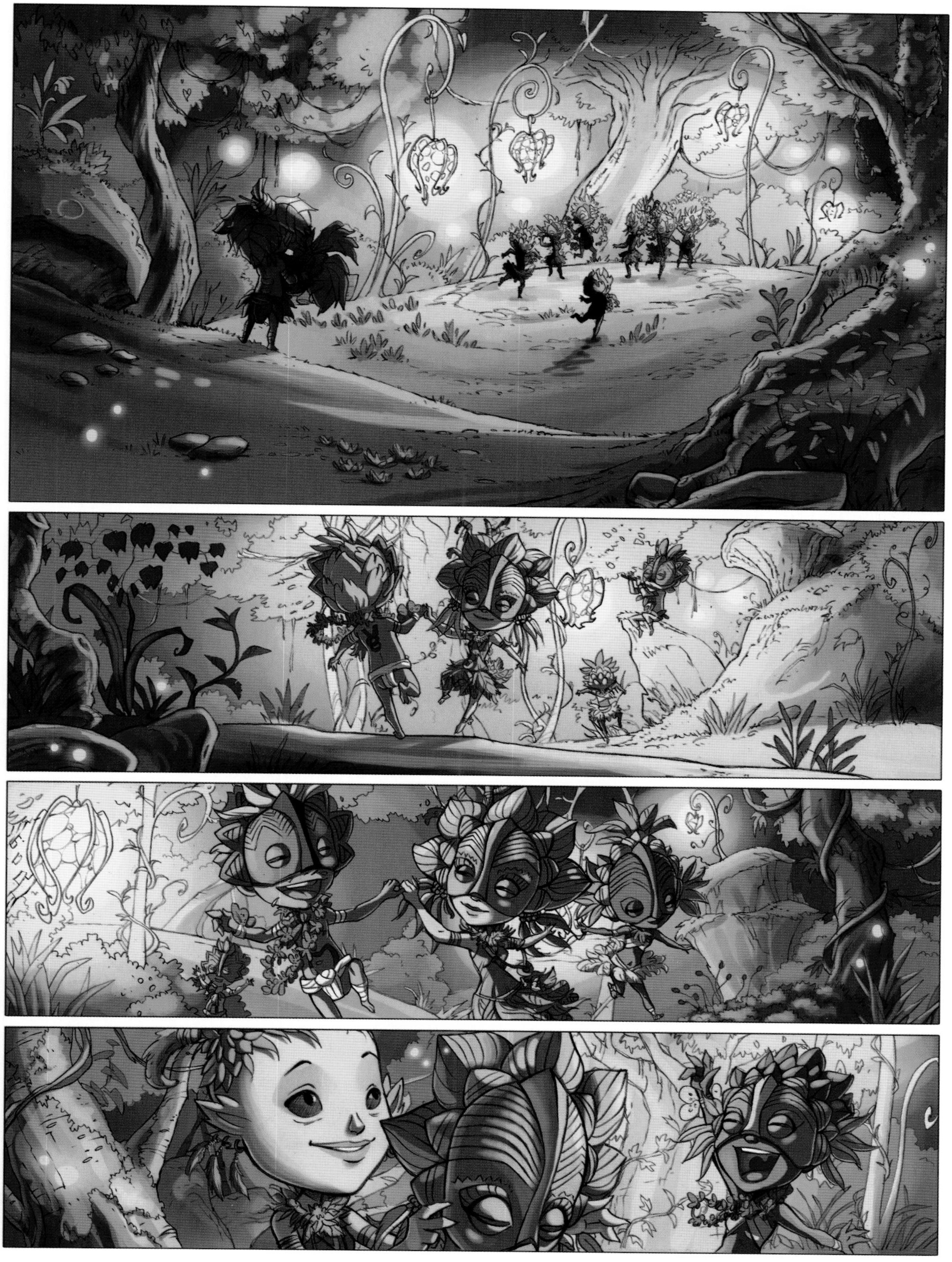

> OH, NATURA, DAZZLING BEAUTY IN THE SUN'S PALE GLOW, MORE THAN THE STAR OF THE DAY, IT'S YOUR SPLENDOR THAT BLINDS ME.

> OH, HOW PRETTY! BUT WHO...?

> NATURA, FRAGRANT FLOWER, MAY OUR HANDS ENTWINE LIKE TENDRILS?

WHO COULD MY SECRET POET BE?

NO, COME BACK! DON'T BE SO SHY! WAIT...!

AH...

WE HAVE TO GO NOW, CLICK...

THERE'S NO TIME TO LOSE!

I AGREE.

WAIT! AN ANSWER FROM TALAMUS!

HM, I SEE. HE ORDERS ME TO CROSS THE FINGERS OF THE LEFT HAND... I CANNOT DISOBEY A DIRECT ORDER.

YES YOU CAN! YOU HAVE TO TAKE US TO TALAMUS FIRST! THE GIANT MIGHT DIE AT ANY MOMENT...

SORRY, NATURA, BUT ORDERS ARE ORDERS. AND THIS ORDER FROM TALAMUS HAS TOP PRIORITY.

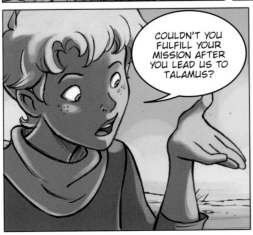

COULDN'T YOU FULFILL YOUR MISSION AFTER YOU LEAD US TO TALAMUS?

WHEN I RETURN, WE CAN SOLVE THE MYSTERY OF MAILBOXES. BE PATIENT!

YOUR BLIND OBEDIENCE WILL KILL US ALL, CLICK!

DON'T BE TOO HARSH ON HIM; HE'S JUST TRYING TO DO THE RIGHT THING. IS THERE ANY WAY WE CAN REACH TALAMUS OURSELVES?

NO, ONLY CLICK KNOWS THE WAY TO THE BRAIN... AND WE'RE LOSING TIME!

CLICK--YOU FOOL!

ANOTHER EARTHQUAKE?

NO, IT'S SOMETHING DIFFERENT...

INSECTS?

DON'T WORRY, THEY'RE HARMLESS!

WONDERFUL! THAT'S ALL WE NEED.

UH, ARE YOU SURE ABOUT THAT, NATURA? THEY'RE HEADING RIGHT AT US!

WHAT'S WRONG WITH THESE INSECTS? WHY ARE THEY ATTACKING US?

I...DON'T KNOW...UP TILL NOW, THEY'VE ONLY BEEN INTERESTED IN POLLEN!

DON'T TAKE THIS THE WRONG WAY, BUT YOUR PLANET IS GETTING WORSE BY THE SECOND!

THEY MUST BE LOOKING FOR WATER!

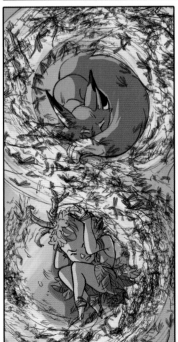

WHAT CAN WE DO? I DON'T WANT TO HURT THEM...

WE'VE GOT TO GET OUT OF HERE!

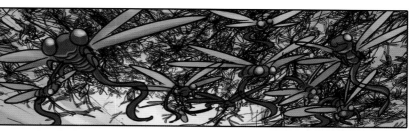

LOOK-- CLICK'S BACK!

YOU ARRIVED JUST IN TIME!

SO I SEE!

CLUCK!

HOW DID YOU DRIVE THE INSECTS AWAY?

I CONCOCTED AN INSECT REPELLENT BASED ON SAND. DON'T BE SURPRISED! AS SUPERVISOR, I HAVE A FEW TRICKS UP MY SLEEVE.

LIKE FINDING TALAMUS, RIGHT?

WHY DID YOU COME BACK, CLICK?

WHEN I SET OUT FOR THE LEFT HAND, I REALIZED THAT I COULDN'T RECOGNIZE ANYTHING. SAND WAS EVERYWHERE. BUT THERE'S EVEN WORSE NEWS.

I SAW PEOPLE FROM EVERY REGION ON THE GIANT, MORE PEOPLE THAN I COULD COUNT, FLEEING THE ENCROACHING DESERT.

OUR PEOPLE ARE SUFFERING SO MUCH THAT THEY HAVE TO LEAVE THEIR HOMES TO LOOK FOR WATER. UNTIL THAT MOMENT, I DIDN'T REALIZE HOW SERIOUS THINGS WERE. THE WHOLE PLANET IS BECOMING A HUGE DESERT!

THEN THIS STRANGE BIRD APPEARED, AND I FOLLOWED IT STRAIGHT BACK TO YOU.

THOSE INSECTS WERE LOOKING FOR WATER TOO... YOUR SWEAT MUST HAVE ATTRACTED THEM.

WE CAN'T WAIT ANY LONGER. WE HAVE TO LEAVE NOW! WHAT DO YOU SAY, FOX, SHALL WE BRING THE WOOD-CLUCKER ALONG?

YOU'RE A REAL MAGICIAN, LITTLE PRINCE!

ALL ABOARD!

WELL, THIS IS NEW.

CLUCK!

QUICK!

GOOD. ACCORDING TO TALAMUS, TO REACH THE BRAIN, WE HAVE TO FOLLOW THE WATER...

WHAT? DON'T YOU KNOW EXACTLY HOW TO GET THERE?

WELL, SORT OF... TALAMUS LOVES TO BE MYSTERIOUS, BUT I KNOW WATER IS THE SIGNPOST.

CLUCK CLUCK!

GOOD RIDDANCE! SHE FINALLY UNDERSTOOD!

DON'T CROW TOO SOON, FOX! WE HAVE TO FOLLOW HER. SHE'S NO ORDINARY CHICKEN!

DOWN THERE!

IT'S THAT SALTY LAKE! BLEAH--I CAN STILL TASTE IT!

SHE JUMPED!

SHOULD WE JUMP TOO?

WHAT ABOUT THE WATER?

THERE WAS WATER HERE, BUT THE GIANT HAS CRIED ALL HIS TEARS...THE LAKE BED IS DRY!

WELL, LET'S MEET AT THE BOTTOM!

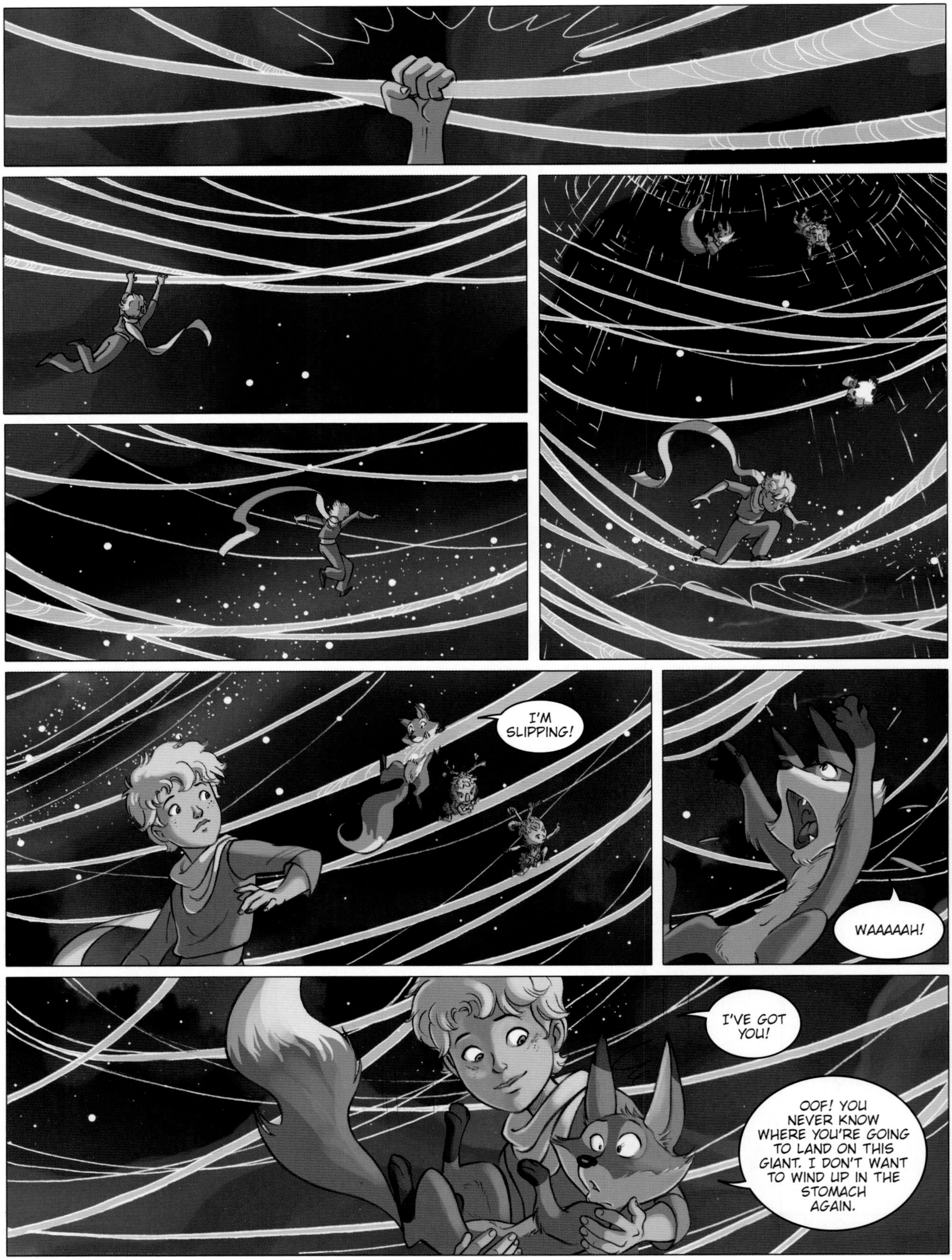
I'M SLIPPING!
WAAAAAH!
I'VE GOT YOU!
OOF! YOU NEVER KNOW WHERE YOU'RE GOING TO LAND ON THIS GIANT. I DON'T WANT TO WIND UP IN THE STOMACH AGAIN.

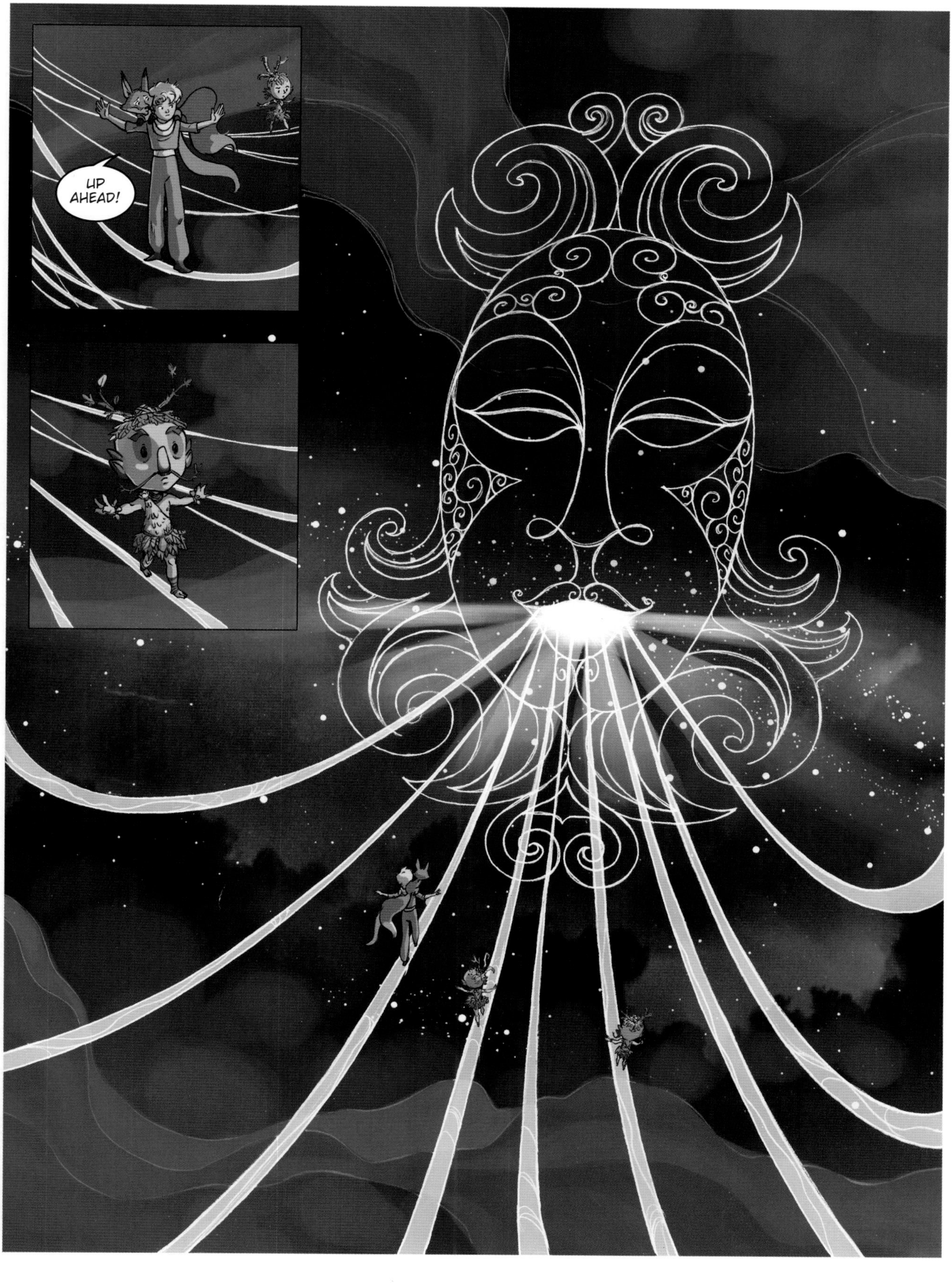
UP AHEAD!

AAAAH!

CLICK! NA... NATURA?

TALAMUS, YOU INCOMPETENT FOOL!

HOW CAN YOU BE SO IRRESPONSIBLE? AREN'T YOU AWARE OF THE GIANT'S CONDITION? WHAT HAVE YOU BEEN DOING?

I...I... I'M SORRY. I...

WHAT'S THAT THING?

IT'S MY FRIEND THE SNAKE. HE HELPS ME WITH MY POEMS...

POEMS? WHAT POEMS?! WHAT'S GOING ON HERE?

NATURA, DON'T BE TOO HARD ON HIM. THE REAL CULPRIT HERE IS THE SNAKE.

BEWARE, TALAMUS! HE'S TRYING TO SEPARATE YOU FROM NATURA... HSSS!

TALAMUS, SEE HOW THE SNAKE USED YOU. HE HAS DISTRACTED YOU FROM YOUR DUTY, AND NOW THE GIANT IS DYING...

WE'VE BEEN TRYING TO GET HOLD OF YOU FOR DAYS.

REALLY? I DIDN'T KNOW-- I PROMISE!

NATURA IS RIGHT. ON THE SURFACE, EVERYTHING IS DRYING UP. THE GIANT IS BECOMING A DESERT... YOUR WORLD IS BEING DESTROYED!

HSSS... HOW DARE YOU DISTRACT TALAMUS FROM HIS POEMS? DON'T YOU UNDERSTAND ANYTHING ABOUT LOVE AND POETRY?

OH, NO! WHAT A NIGHTMARE! I'VE BEEN SO STUPID!

DO WHAT YOU WANT, TALAMUSSS. YOU'LL BE SSSORRY...

ARE YOU OKAY?

YES...BUT WE MUST ACT QUICKLY!

CLICK, SEND THIS CARD TO THE LIVER. NATURA, WRITE AN ORDER TELLING THE STOMACH TO ACTIVATE ITS EMERGENCY ENZYMES.

IT'S HORRIBLE! THE BRAIN-- IT'S ROTTING AWAY!

DON'T GO NEAR IT!

YOU, LITTLE BEASTIE, GO FIND ME SOME NEW TABLETS! WHEN YOU HAVE THEM--

AAAAAH!

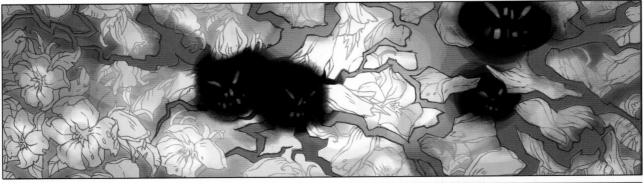

ALL THE ORGANS ARE STARTING TO FAIL! THE END IS NEAR!

TALAMUS, STEP BACK!

AHHH... FEEL THAT BREEZE!

CLICK IS GOING TO BE HAPPY!

THE LUNGS ARE WORKING AGAIN! THAT WAS CLOSE!

LITTLE PRINCE, YOU'VE SAVED US! THANK YOU!

THE HEARTBEAT HAS RETURNED TO NORMAL!

BOOM BOOM BOOM BOOM

HOORAY!

THE BEST WAY TO THANK ME IS TO NURSE THE GIANT BACK TO HEALTH.

WE'LL GIVE YOU ALL THE HELP YOU NEED, TALAMUS.

YOU CAN COUNT ON ME.

THANKS, MY FRIENDS.

NATURA, I MUST SPEAK WITH YOU.

YOU? I HAD NO IDEA...

ON THE DAY OF THE SPRING BALL, SOMEONE RECITED A POEM TO YOU. IT WAS ME!

I WAS AFRAID. I DIDN'T DARE TELL YOU HOW I FELT. BUT I LOVE YOU, NATURA...

THE POET HAD A MASK...

SO...IT REALLY WAS YOU.

NATURA, WILL YOU MARRY ME?

Y-YES!

THANK YOU, LITTLE PRINCE!

WELL, I'VE FLOWN THE COOP AT LAST!

OH, I THOUGHT YOU AND THE WOOD-CLUCKER MADE QUITE A PAIR OF LOVEBIRDS!

THE END

The Little Prince

AS IMAGINED BY

DIDIER CONVARD

&

PHILIPPE ADAMOV

COLORING
GREG SALSEDO

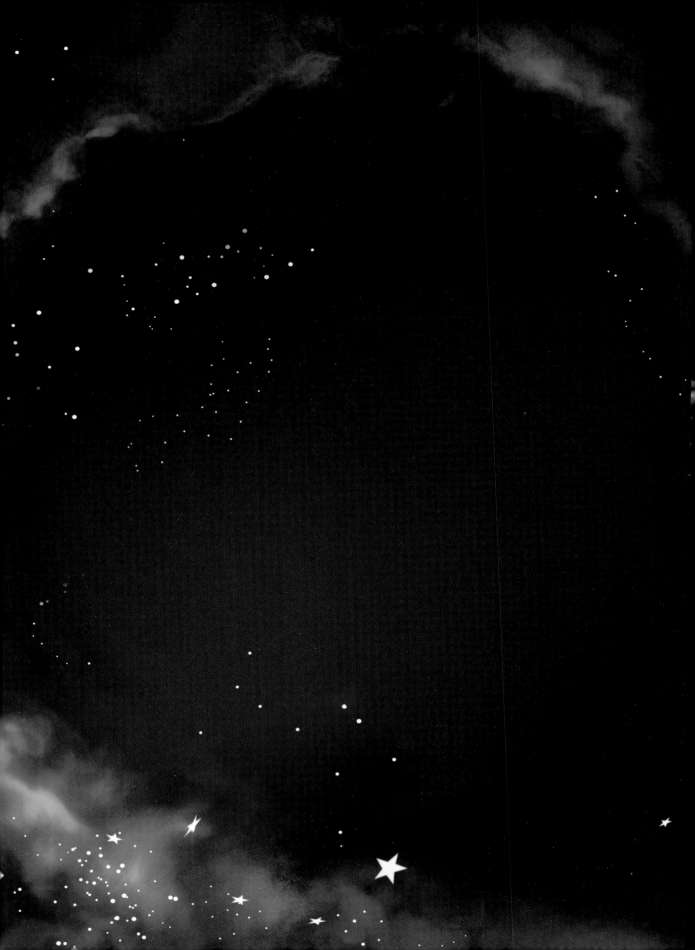

YET ANOTHER NEW PLANET FOR THE LITTLE PRINCE TO EXPLORE. THE GENTLE TOUCH OF A COOL BREEZE SOFTLY CARESSES THE GRASS. THE SCENT OF EXOTIC HERBS AND SPICES WAFTS THROUGH THE AIR.

THIS IS MY FAVORITE PART OF EVERY JOURNEY: DISCOVERING A WONDROUS NEW WORLD CREATED BY SOME GREAT ARCHITECT THAT WE CANNOT EVEN BEGIN TO UNDERSTAND.

HOW IRKSOME! WHY CAN'T HUMANS JUST APPRECIATE WHATEVER THEY ENCOUNTER WITHOUT OVERTHINKING EVERYTHING!

THIS PLANET IS INHABITED! I'VE BEEN A BIT SAD HAVING ONLY TWO FRIENDS, YOU AND ROSE. NOW I CAN HAVE OTHER ACQUAINTANCES TO ENRICH MY CONVERSATIONS.

HOW UNGRATEFUL! TWO REALLY CLOSE FRIENDS SHOULD BE WORTH MORE THAN A WHOLE ARMY OF PEOPLE TO CHAT WITH.

WHAT'S GOING ON?

IT'S AS IF WE'RE INVISIBLE. THEY DON'T NOTICE US AT ALL! NO GREETINGS! NO SIGNS OF WELCOME!

BIG SURPRISE! DOES HE THINK TRUE FRIENDSHIPS GROW LIKE DANDELIONS IN THE PARK?

A CITY! AT LAST WE'LL FIND SOME PEOPLE WHO WILL TALK WITH US! THEY CAN TELL US THE NAME OF THIS FINE PLANET, AND WE CAN FIND OUT HOW WE'RE SIMILAR AND HOW WE'RE DIFFERENT. IMAGINE WHAT WE'LL LEARN!

WHY BOTHER? NO ONE'S PERFECT--WE'LL JUST BE DISAPPOINTED IN NEW WAYS.

51

WHAT A FEAST FOR OUR SENSES! A KALEIDOSCOPE OF COLORS! INTOXICATING PERFUMES AND DELICATE FRAGRANCES! THE MURMUR OF A THOUSAND VOICES BLENDING INTO A MELODY AS CAPTIVATING AS THE SORCERER'S ENCHANTMENT!

HOW EASILY ENTERTAINED! HE'S LIKE A CHILD BEGUILED BY A PUPPET SHOW OR A NEW TYPE OF CANDY.

EXCUSE ME, WOULD YOU PLEASE TELL ME THE NAME OF THIS PLANET? MY FOX AND I ARE FROM ASTEROID B612, A SMALL PLANET NOT NEARLY AS IMPRESSIVE AS YOURS...

MIGHT I TROUBLE YOU FOR AN ANSWER TO MY QUESTION? WHAT KIND OF ADULTS ARE YOU? DON'T YOU REALIZE THAT IT'S COMMON COURTESY FOR ADULTS TO ANSWER A CHILD'S QUESTION?

HOW DISAPPOINTING! NO DEFERENCE TO VISITING ROYALTY AT ALL!

WILL YOU LET ME JOIN YOUR GAME?

HOPE SPRINGS ETERNAL!

I DON'T UNDERSTAND. NO ONE WILL PAY US THE SLIGHTEST ATTENTION!

WHAT A BLOW TO OUR SELF-ESTEEM!

EVEN CHILDREN MY OWN AGE IGNORE ME! EVERYONE HERE MUST BE EITHER PROUD OR PRETENTIOUS!

VANITY OF VANITIES, ALL IS VANITY!

NIGHT FALLS SO QUICKLY HERE, AND WITH SUCH A CHILL! ALL OF A SUDDEN, I'M NEARLY FROZEN!

WHAT A BAD OMEN!

WHAT'S HAPPENING, FOX? WHERE DID THE CITY GO? WHERE ARE ALL THE PEOPLE? IT'S SO DARK!

HOW CREEPY!

HELLO? HELLO?

AH, IF I HAD ONLY KNOWN I HAD VISITORS...

WHO ARE YOU? CAN YOU TELL ME WHAT JUST HAPPENED, SIR? EVERYTHING WAS WONDERFUL, BUT...

THEN I WOKE UP! AS I SAID, IF I HAD ONLY KNOWN I HAD VISITORS, I WOULD HAVE STAYED ASLEEP.

I DON'T UNDERSTAND.

NOTHING COULD BE SIMPLER, MY BOY! I AM THE LAST PRIEST MNEMOS, THE SOLE SURVIVOR OF A CALAMITY THAT DESTROYED ONE OF THE MOST MAGNIFICENT PLANETS IN THE GALAXY! FOR TWO CENTURIES, METEORITES RAINED DOWN UPON OUR CITIES, OUR AZEROID PONDS, OUR MAGNOFLUX FIELDS...

FOR TWO CENTURIES? SO YOU MUST BE...

VERY, VERY OLD. IN FACT, I BET YOU'RE WONDERING WHAT A PRIEST MNEMOS IS, AREN'T YOU? WELL, IT'S A PERSON WITH A PERFECT MEMORY, WHO CAN REMEMBER EVERYTHING. EVERYTHING! THE WAY A GRASSHOPPER'S ANTENNAE SHIVER IN THE WIND, THE DELICATE HUE OF A ROSY PEARL. MEN, WOMEN, CHILDREN! BUILDINGS, BLADES OF GRASS, EVEN DUST FLOATING IN THE AIR! I REMEMBER EVERY SINGLE DETAIL OF MY DOOMED PLANET!

AND I HAVE THE POWER TO PROJECT IMAGES FROM MY MEMORY, TO RE-CREATE THEM IN ALL THEIR GLORY--THEIR COLORS, SOUNDS, TEXTURES, AND FRAGRANCES! WHEN I SLEEP, MY MEMORY AWAKENS, AND I DREAM MY WONDERFUL WORLD BACK INTO EXISTENCE. THAT'S WHY I SLEEP SO OFTEN...

MY FOX AND I ARE SORRY TO HAVE DISTURBED YOU, SIR. WE'LL BE ON OUR WAY SO YOU CAN GO BACK TO SLEEP.

TO SLEEP... YES, TO REMEMBER...

I REALIZE NOW WHY NO ONE WOULD TALK TO US. THEY LIVED A LONG TIME AGO, BEFORE WE EVER SET FOOT ON THIS PLANET.

NEVER FORGET, LITTLE TRAVELER, THAT MEMORY ALWAYS TRIUMPHS OVER DEATH! NEVER FORGET!

ANTOINE DE SAINT-EXUPÉRY
Aviator • Author • Adventurer • Hero

Antoine de Saint-Exupéry, author of the novel *The Little Prince* on which these adventures are based, was born on June 29, 1900, in Lyon, France. He was the [?]d of five children: Marie-Madeleine, Simone, Antoine, François, and Gabrielle. It [wa]s when he was twelve years old, during his summer break from boarding school, [tha]t airplanes and flying first made a huge impression on him.

In 1920, he was accepted into the École des Beaux-Arts in Paris to study [arch]itecture, but the next year he joined the Second Aviation Regiment of the armed [forc]es and received his pilot's license. In 1922, he had his first plane crash and suffered [a h]ead fracture. He had to leave the armed forces and work at different jobs on the [gro]und to earn a living.

By May of 1926, Saint-Exupéry was able to fly again. He delivered airmail, which [wa]s a new and sometimes dangerous profession, on routes from France to Senegal and [all t]he way to South America. That was where, in 1931, he met and married Consuelo [Su]ncin.

From 1933 to 1938, Saint-Exupéry was very busy. He traveled to North Africa [and] Indochina and attempted to break the flight speed record from Paris to Saigon, [Viet]nam—during which his plane crashed again. It went down in the middle of the [Sah]ara Desert. After his recovery, his life became even busier. He wrote newspaper [rep]orts in Spain on the Spanish Civil War, scouted airplane routes between Casablanca [and] Timbuktu, wrote a screenplay, registered several patents, and traveled to the [Uni]ted States. In 1939, with the start of World War II, he returned to France and [talk]ed his way into a job as a high-risk reconnaissance pilot for the French Air Force. [But] this only lasted until France reached an armistice agreement with Germany.

In December 1940, Saint-Exupéry returned to visit friends in New York, where [he fi]nally began work on *The Little Prince.* The story is narrated by a pilot who has [cras]hed his plane into the Sahara Desert. He meets a little prince visiting from a [fara]way asteroid. Along the way, the prince also meets Fox and Snake. By late 1942, [afte]r spending the spring and summer writing and illustrating, Saint-Exupéry had [com]pleted his novel, and in April 1943 it was published in his native language of French [(Le] Petit Prince) and in English.

Saint-Exupéry was eager to return to the war. He decided to join the Free French [for]ces in Algeria, who were continuing the fight against the Axis powers. Because of [his] age, at first he had a hard time convincing them to let him fly. He was authorized [to fl]y five dangerous missions. In fact, he flew eight. On July 31, 1944, Saint-Exupéry [wen]t on a scouting flight to prepare for military landings in the south of France. His [plan]e disappeared over the water, and he was never seen again.

Over the decades since *The Little Prince* was published, it has gone on to become one [of th]e best-selling novels of all time. In 2003, a small moon in our solar system's asteroid [belt] was named Petit-Prince in honor of the masterpiece Saint-Exupéry created.

The Little Prince in the Twenty-First Century

The Little Prince is a landmark of literature and one of the most translated an[d] beloved books in the world. It tackles universal topics with a unique philosophic[al] and poetic sensibility. Sixty-five years after the first edition, the Saint-Exupé[ry] Estate decided to bring the character back for a whole new generation . . . and f[or] everyone who has ever loved the boy who sees the world with his heart.

The Little Prince now returns in a series of new adventures that remain tru[e] to the spirit of the original work. He will travel from planet to planet chasing th[e] wicked Snake, who wants to plunge the whole universe into darkness. On eac[h] planet, the Snake sends bad thoughts into the minds of its inhabitants, makin[g] them sad and grim, draining the life out of their planet. The Little Prince mu[st] leave his beautiful Rose behind and must use his vision and courage to defeat th[e] Snake, bringing along his friend Fox to save planets in danger across the univers[e.]

About the Adapters

After several years in video games and Japanese animation, adapt[er] Guillaume Dorison became literary editor for the publisher Les Humanoïd[es] Associés in 2006, where he launched the Shogun Collection dedicated to origin[al] manga. In June 2010, he founded Élyum Studio with Didier Poli, Jean-Baptist[e] Hostache, and Xavier Dorison to provide services for the creation of graph[ic] novels. In addition to his position as director of writing for Élyum Studio, [he] has more than two dozen comics and manga to his credit under the pseudony[m] IZU, has written several titles in the Explora series on world explorers for Frenc[h] publisher Glénat, and won the 2010 Animeland Prize for best French manga.

Didier Poli, artistic director for the new graphic novel adaptations based o[n] *The Little Prince*, was born in Lyon in 1971. After graduate studies in appli[ed] arts, he worked for various animation studios including Disney. He was worki[ng] as artistic director for the video game company Kalisto Entertainment when [he] met Manuel Bichebois in 2001 and began drawing Bichebois's graphic novel seri[es] L'Enfant de l'orage. At the 2004 Nîmes Festival, Didier Poli received the Bron[ze] Boar prize for young talent. He continues, along with his work on graphic novel[s,] to work regularly in cartoons and video games as a designer and storyboard artis[t.]

Book 1: The Planet of Wind

Book 2: The Planet of the Firebird

Book 3: The Planet of Music

Book 4: The Planet of Jade

Book 5: The Star Snatcher's Planet

Book 6: The Planet of the Night Globes

Book 7: The Planet of the Overhearers

Book 8: The Planet of the Tortoise Driver

Book 9: The Planet of the Giant

Book 10: The Planet of Trainiacs

Book 11: The Planet of Libris

Book 12: The Planet of Ludokaa

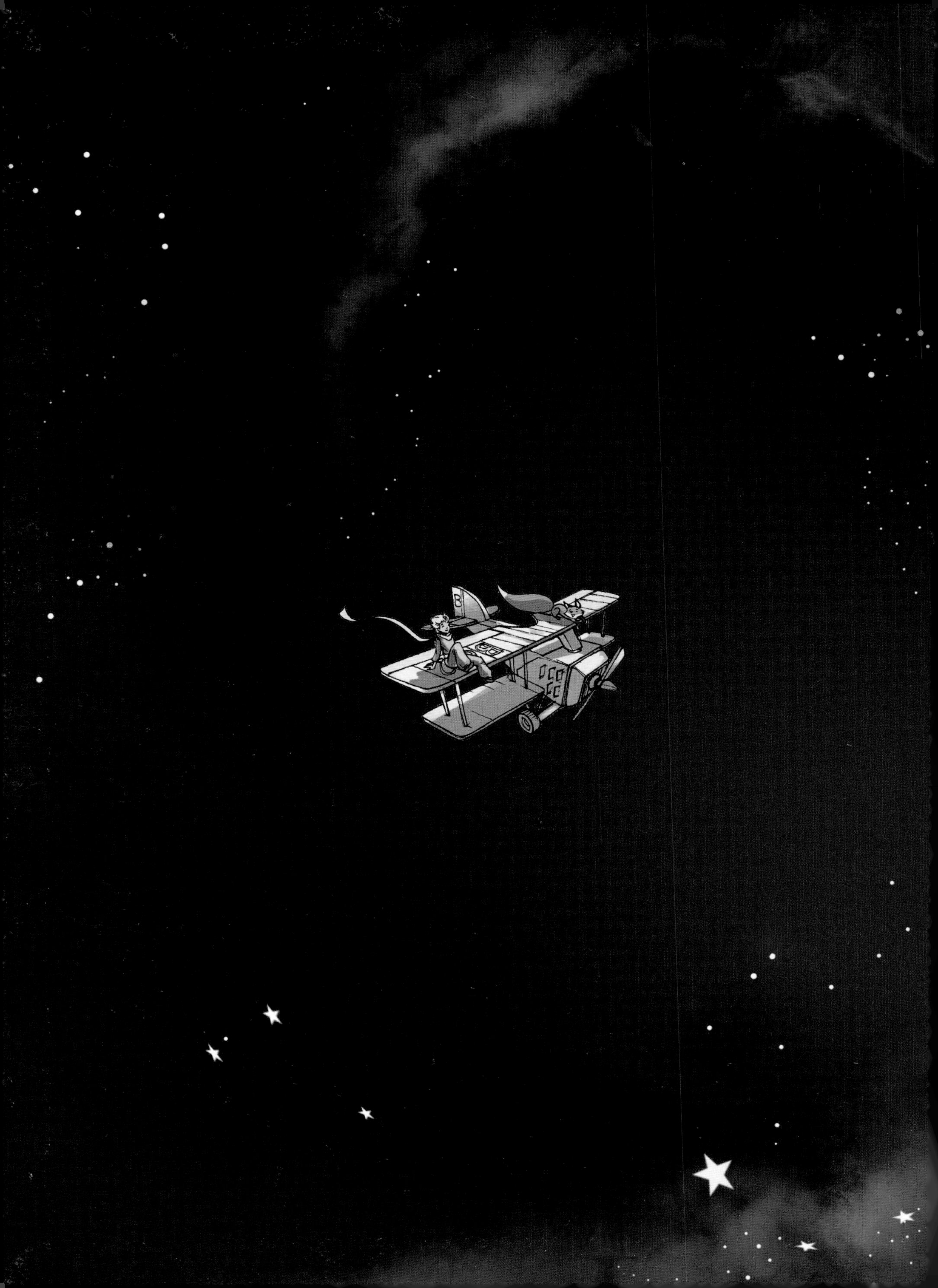